Silverlake Fairy School

Wands and Charms

Silverlake
Fairy School

A magical world
where fairy dreams come true

Silverlake Fairy School

Wands and Charms

Elizabeth Lindsay

Illustrated by Anna Currey

USBORNE

For J.S., H.L. and J.G.

They know who they are.

First published in 2009 by Usborne Publishing Ltd., Usborne House,
83-85 Saffron Hill, London EC1N 8RT, England.
www.usborne.com

Text copyright © Elizabeth Lindsay, 2009

Illustration copyright © Usborne Publishing Ltd., 2009

A CIP catalogue record for this book is available from the British Library.

UK ISBN 9780746076811 First published in America in 2011 AE.
American ISBN 9780794530631 JFM MJJASOND/11 01559/1
Printed in Dongguan, Guangdong, China.

Contents

Chapter One

All Aboard

L ila had been dreaming of Silverlake Fairy School
ever since she had passed the entrance test.
It had been a long wait but the first day of school
had arrived, and here she was on the riverbank
surrounded by her friends and the other First
Year fairies, ready to go. She was brimming with
excitement. The school was on an island on the
far side of the Great Silver Lake, and to reach it
they had to travel up the River of Sparkling
Waters. *The Golden Queen*, the glittering royal

barge belonging to the Fairy King and Queen, was to take them there.

The Fairy Palace had always been Lila's home. Here was everything she knew and loved. She held tight to Cook's hand. Soon they would be saying goodbye for the first time since Lila was a baby. She felt homesick at the thought. If only Cook could come too.

The autumn morning was chilly and the royal party was late. Fairies rubbed their fingers and wiggled their toes to keep warm. Lila hopped from one foot to another, fluttering her purple wings. They couldn't go anywhere until Princess Bee Balm was aboard. It was her first day at Silverlake Fairy School as well.

There was a flurry among the waiting fairies as six prancing white ponies arrived, pulling the royal coach. The driver, an elf in green-and-gold livery, spoke soothingly to steady his team. They had galloped the short journey across the meadow from the Fairy Palace and couldn't understand why they were stopping so soon.

"Better late than never," said Cook huffily.

"It's going to be ages before we see you again, Lila," said Mip, the shoeshine elf and Lila's good friend.

"Mustn't spoil the moment by getting soppy," Cook said, with a catch in her voice. "You going to school is what I've always dreamed of, Lila. But I will miss you something rotten."

"Me too," groaned Mip.

"I'll miss you both terribly and horribly," said Lila, giving Cook a big hug and Mip a kiss on the cheek. The elf turned bright pink but looked pleased all the same.

A footman opened the carriage door and the Fairy King and Queen stepped onto the grass. Those waiting bowed and curtsied. Eager young eyes took in every detail of the beautiful Princess who followed. There were gasps and applause.

Wands and Charms

Princess Bee Balm was wrapped in a willow-wool cloak of the purest white. From underneath peeked a pink frock, interwoven with threads of fairy gold and silver, that matched the glitter in her pale pink hair. The Princess smiled and, with a graceful nod, acknowledged the greetings.

Lila's new frock matched her wings and hair to perfection and, although she would never have as many clothes as the Princess, today she felt her equal. The dress was a special "going to school" present from Cook and all the other fairies and elves who worked in the kitchen; her tattered old blue one had been dumped in the trash and was gone forever. For once, Lila felt like a princess herself.

"A fair-weather charm," ordered the King. "We can't send the little ones to school in this gloom."

The Lord Chamberlain, stately and dressed in black, stepped forward and raised his silver snake wand. A charm streaked into the sky and spun

All Aboard

among the heavy gray clouds until the weak autumn sun broke through. *The Golden Queen* glinted and flamed in the watery light. A large trunk belonging to Princess Bee Balm was carried up the gangplank and placed with the other fairies' luggage on the deck.

"All aboard!" the helmsman cried and the elf-oarsmen took a firm grip on their oars.

Lila's friends from the palace kitchen gathered around her and kissed her goodbye until, last of all, she was swept into one of Cook's bear hugs. It hid the tears that welled up for both of them. Mip solemnly whispered a reminder in her ear.

"Watch out for the Princess!"

Lila nodded. Princess Bee Balm had tried to stop her, a mere kitchen fairy, from passing the Silverlake Fairy School entrance test. She wasn't going to like Lila any better now that they were both going to the same school. Lila would *definitely* watch out for the Princess!

Wands and Charms

Princess Bee Balm walked regally aboard the shimmering barge and even the golden queen figurehead appeared to turn her head to watch. The new pupils curtsied low. The Princess made her way across the deck and entered the golden cabin. Through the windows, which were open to the air, she could be seen making herself comfortable upon a golden throne. There was a hustle and bustle to be the first on behind the Princess and get a place close to her. Lila waited until the last minute, giving Cook one final hug, before she tripped up the gangplank, her friends waving her aboard.

Lila looked across the river that she loved. She had swum in its sparkling waters often enough and had once, daringly, run her hand along the beaten gold planking of the royal barge as it glided past, wondering what it would be like to sail in such a proud vessel. And now she was.

The helmsman gave his orders and the mooring

ropes were cast off. The great boat drifted away from the riverbank and, to the beat of a drum, the oars dipped into the water and began to pull them upstream.

"Goodbye," Lila called. "Goodbye." There was a tug at her heart and she didn't stop waving until Cook, Mip and her other friends had become a blur of tiny figures. She felt sad to be leaving, but happy to be going too. It was the start of a great adventure.

"What a lot of friends you've got," said a yellow-ocher fairy coming to stand next to her.

"Yes, but I live at the palace," said Lila, dabbing her eyes and smiling. "It was easy for everyone to come and wave goodbye."

"Are you a royal fairy too?"

"No," Lila laughed. "But it feels like it now that I'm wearing a new frock and my Silverlake Fairy School bracelet." She shook the silver chain up her arm. The yellow-ocher fairy was wearing an identical bracelet. It was a sign that they had both been accepted at Silverlake Fairy School.

"My name's Lilac Blossom, Lila for short. What's yours?"

"Nutmeg. Meggie, to my friends."

"Hi, Meggie."

"Hi, Lila." Both fairies smiled and Lila said, "I work in the great kitchen at the Fairy Palace, or I did until today. Cook brought me up. I'm an orphan, you see. It was her dearest wish that I go to Silverlake Fairy School. And mine too. So I took the entrance test. What about you?"

"My parents come from the Spice Islands in the Ocean of Diamond Waters, but now we live on the mainland by the seashore."

"How wonderful," said Lila. "I've always wanted to swim in the sea."

"Swim!" Meggie shivered. "I never swim. My parents want me to learn Spice Islands' charms but that would mean sailing there. I don't even like being on the river. Imagine having to go on a sea voyage!"

"Are the Spice Islands that far away?" asked Lila.

"They're too far for flying," said Meggie. She gently stroked the fabric of Lila's dress. "This is beautiful gossamer. I've never seen such a deep purple before. But then I've never met a purple fairy before either."

"Cook had to have the gossamer specially woven. No one wants to wear such a dark color except me. I think I must be the only purple fairy in the Kingdom."

"And it's such a fine thread!" said Meggie. "When I leave school I want to weave gossamer and make clothes, ballgowns, hats, gloves and shawls." Her eyes shone at the thought.

"Would you make them for me?" asked Lila. "I will always need clothes specially made if I want to wear this color. Would you?"

All Aboard

"It will be an honor."

The two fairies beamed at each other and Lila felt she had made a friend.

"You must know the Princess well if you work at the palace," Meggie said. "I'd love to get to know her. She's very beautiful. And that willow-wool cloak is heaven."

"Beautiful she is," agreed Lila. "Friendly she isn't, so, no, I can't say I know her at all really."

"But she's very popular," said Meggie. "I'm surprised you're not her friend. Look, she's surrounded by all the other fairies on the barge. Why don't we join them inside the cabin and say hello?"

"You go," said Lila, "but I think I'll stay here if you don't mind."

"Oh," said Meggie, surprised.

"I just love watching the sun on the water," explained Lila. "It's making the ripples into little lights. Do you see?"

Wands and Charms

In the golden cabin, the Princess was entertaining her listeners with stories of her many trips aboard *The Golden Queen*. She had voyaged as far as the Spice Islands and had once accompanied her parents on a royal visit to Silverlake Fairy School. Her confident voice carried on the breeze. She was the center of attention, with her audience hanging on her every word. Then the Princess caught Lila's eye. Lila hadn't meant to be noticed and turned quickly away.

With an elegant swoop, her cloak ballooning in the breeze, Princess Bee Balm stepped from the cabin and crossed the main deck, her admirers hurrying after her. Meggie curtsied.

"Lilac Blossom, you're in the way. I want to show everyone how fast the barge travels upriver. Buzz off, will you?"

"See what I mean? Not very friendly at all," whispered Lila into Meggie's ear. Meggie looked confused.

All Aboard

"Don't you know it's rude to whisper?" snapped the Princess. "I can see that Cooky hasn't taught you any manners. What did you say?"

"Nothing important," said Lila, sensing a quarrel and moving off as she'd been told.

The Princess turned her attention to Meggie, all smiles now.

"And what's your name? We haven't yet met."

"Nutmeg, Your Highness," replied Meggie.

"I love your hair," the Princess continued. "It's the color of autumn leaves. Very pretty."

Meggie smiled happily at the compliment.

"Look at how fast we're speeding upstream, everyone, even though the elves are rowing against the current. And the river widens here." All the fairies, including Meggie, obediently followed the Princess's gaze to the whirls and eddies of the barge's wake and then to the far riverbank.

Lila wandered further along the deck out of the way. It was a shame that Meggie seemed to have been swept up in the Princess's entourage, but Lila supposed she was going to have to get used to this sort of thing happening.

"Oh, Nutmeg," exclaimed the Princess, laughing brightly. "How silly you are! You're wearing your school bracelet on the wrong wrist."

On hearing Meggie's name, Lila was all attention.

"No, no, Your Majesty," said Meggie. "I was told in my acceptance letter to wear it on this arm."

"That can't be right," said Princess Bee Balm. "Everyone else has their bracelet on the other wrist. Change it at once." Lila was curious to see what Meggie would do. "Go on, switch it over."

"But…" Meggie looked stricken.

"You heard what I said. Don't you think she should change it over, everyone?"

A chorus of yeses greeted this question.

"No," said Lila.

The Princess ignored the one "no," and Meggie

All Aboard

appeared too flustered to hear what Lila had said. Reluctantly, she slipped the bracelet from one wrist to the other. She gave a little yelp and rubbed her arm as though it hurt.

"Oh, stop making such a fuss," Princess Bee Balm said. "The bracelet looks much better like that. Now you're the same as everyone else."

She turned away and the other fairies followed, leaving Meggie pale and holding her arm. Lila darted over.

"Put it back how it was. I think you should."

Meggie tried to do as Lila suggested but slid to the deck with a whimper.

"Meggie?" said Lila. "What's the matter?"

"I feel peculiar," Meggie said. Lila quickly slipped the bracelet from Meggie's wrist. Meggie blinked and shook her head. "What a weird feeling that was. It's going now."

"Put the bracelet on how you were told to wear it," said Lila. She dropped the chain into Meggie's palm and Meggie slipped it back onto her right wrist.

"What do you think you're doing, Lilac Blossom?" The Princess's voice cut the air and she looked furious.

"Oh, no, here we go," Lila groaned under her breath. "It looks like Princess Bee Balm is going to do her best to spoil our first day at Silverlake Fairy School. Meggie, watch out!"

Chapter Two

The Island in the Lake

Lila quickly helped Meggie up.

"You've changed your bracelet back when I told you to wear it like the rest of us," said Princess Bee Balm.

Meggie ignored her and squeezed Lila's arm. "Thank you for helping me, Lila. I feel quite all right again now." She turned slowly to face the Princess. "I'm left-handed, Your Majesty. I must wear my bracelet like this. I don't feel right if I don't."

"You do what I say, not what you think. Trust Lilac Blossom to interfere."

"Nutmeg has done what the school asked her to do," said Lila.

"And I'm telling her to do something else," said the Princess. She smiled a superior smile, expecting to be obeyed.

Lila was furious. "Stop throwing your weight around and leave Nutmeg alone!"

"Mind your own business, Purple Nails," sneered the Princess and turned back to Meggie, expecting her to obey.

"I won't change the bracelet again," Meggie said with gentle authority. "Ordering me won't do any good." A few fairies gasped, and the Princess was left looking foolish. Linking arms with Lila, Meggie turned and walked away. The Princess said something inaudible. Her admirers laughed loudly, making faces at the retreating pair.

"Oh dear," Lila said. "Now we've done it. But I

suppose it could have been worse."

"Not much," said Meggie. "But I've already learned two useful things today. Always to wear my bracelet on my right wrist, and that the most self-important fairy on the boat is the Princess!"

"I already knew that," said Lila. "She didn't like me before today, and she's going to like me even less now. I'm afraid the same's going to apply to you."

"I don't want to be liked by a fairy that unpleasant," said Meggie.

"But now that we've both fallen out with her there may be trouble ahead," said Lila.

"We'll face it together." Meggie's eyes were alight. "As friends?" she asked.

"Yes, as friends," Lila agreed and they huddled together in the bow.

The sunshine conjured up by the Lord Chamberlain's fair-weather charm had been left far behind and now the helmsman was steering into a mist that hung heavily on the water, muffling the beat of the drum. But the elf-oarsmen rowed on steadily. They had lost sight of the riverbanks and Lila guessed they were far out in the middle of the Great Silver Lake.

"On the far side of the water are the Eerie Mountains," said Meggie. "There's a picture of them covered in snow in my Geography book."

"Yes," said Lila. "It's a shame it's so misty. But I guess we'll get to see them one day."

"Boggarts live there," added Meggie.

"Did you read about them too? Nasty, evil creatures," Lila said in a spooky voice, wiggling her fingers.

"Stop it," said Meggie, grinning. "I don't ever want to meet one. They won't be able to get into Silverlake Fairy School, will they?"

"Never," said Lila. "The school wouldn't be there if they could."

"Of course not," agreed Meggie. "Silly of me."

The Island in the Lake

But Lila could see that she wasn't totally reassured.

Ahead, hundreds of tiny fairy lights glowed silver, faintly at first, but with more strength as the barge came closer. An enormous shadowy wall towered above them. The beat of the oarsmen slowed.

"Oh, Lila," said Meggie. "Do you think we've arrived?"

A ripple of anticipation brought the other fairies rushing toward the bow and the Princess was abandoned. They surrounded Lila and Meggie with their chatter. The elves shipped their oars and the barge came to a gentle rest alongside a stone jetty. The looming figure of an ancient dragon caught the mooring lines in his great claws and made the barge secure.

"No rushing," the dragon ordered in a gruff voice, as if expecting all the fairies to race along the gangplank the moment the elves put it in place. When no one moved at all, he inspected them more closely. The First Years were politely waiting for Princess Bee Balm to lead the way. The old dragon became impatient.

"Come on, hurry up," he barked. "I don't have all day."

The Princess gave him a dark look from the top of the gangplank.

"I suppose you know who I am?" she asked.

"An impertinent First Year fairy," said the dragon. "Get a move on."

"I am Princess Bee Balm," she said and waited expectantly. The dragon turned his great head toward her. His faded and scratched scales, and his drooping mouth were sinister in the shadows. One of his teeth had broken off and his right ear was badly torn. He was not a dragon to trifle with.

"I don't care who you are, just get a move on. I won't be telling you again."

The Island in the Lake

Princess Bee Balm shrugged as if to say that this was all that could be expected from such an ignorant creature.

"Follow the lights," he instructed when she got to the bottom of the gangplank.

"Thank you. And what's your name?"

The dragon gave the Princess a quizzical look. "Captain Klop, retired. Now make it snappy."

"There's no need to be rude," said the Princess. "A helping hand please, Captain Klop."

The dragon grunted and held out a claw. The Princess placed her palm upon it and jumped neatly onto the jetty.

"Hurry up, everyone. You heard what Captain Klop said, we don't have all day."

"Follow the lights," he repeated, as the rest of the First Year fairies spilled off after the Princess, laughing and chattering. Lila stepped onto dry land at last and bobbed a curtsy to the dragon. He stared down at her.

"And who might you be?"

"Lilac Blossom."

"Cook's little purple fairy?" he asked.

"Yes," said Lila, surprised that he knew who she was.

"Follow on, Lilac Blossom," he said, almost kindly, and Lila hurried to catch up with Meggie, who was waiting for her.

Flickering lights guided their way along the jetty toward the school and reflections danced on the water. The jetty ended short of the high castle wall, which on closer inspection Lila saw was made of solid silver. A shiny drawbridge spanned the gap, hanging from two glistening chains. When the drawbridge was raised, the gate would be impregnable.

"How wonderful that Silverlake Fairy School is inside a real castle," said Lila. Through the mist she could just make out some battlements and, higher still, the edge of a turret. She ran across

the drawbridge. Meggie caught up to Lila and took her hand.

"Come on," she said. "We must catch up with the others." As they walked under the gatehouse together the hairs on Lila's arm stood on end.

"Did your bracelet tingle?" she asked Meggie.

"Yes, did yours? They must be saying *Welcome to Silverlake Fairy School*."

Rubbing their goosebumps and giggling, they ran into brilliant sunshine and came to a surprised stop.

"The sun's out here!" gasped Lila.

"In a garden," added Meggie.

"With hundreds of fairies!" cried Lila.

"And all of them different colors!" grinned Meggie.

"And there's a pool with a fountain," said Lila, pointing.

"And a forest," laughed Meggie. "Listen to the birdsong."

The Island in the Lake

"It's not at all how I imagined school," Lila said at last. "It's a million times lovelier."

A glittering orange fairy fluttered over to them. Both Lila and Meggie remembered her from the Silverlake Fairy School entrance test. It was Mistress Pipit, who taught the First Years. Pip-it! Lila remembered her telling them how to say her name. Later Cook had told her that the teacher was named after a little bird. Mistress Pipit's smile was warm and friendly.

"My last two pupils," she said, marking them off her list. "It's Lilac Blossom and Nutmeg, isn't it?" Her voice was kind.

"Yes, Mistress Pipit," they said and curtsied politely.

"Welcome to Silverlake Fairy School. I'm sure you'll be very happy here. It's always summer in the garden. You'll soon warm up. Quickly now, join the others. I've much to show you."

Lila's heart leaped with excitement. She was

longing to find out more about this place. Her one regret was that Cook and Mip weren't there to share the adventure with her, but she would write and tell them everything. Meggie squeezed her hand, and together, eyes gleaming, they followed their teacher across shiny cobblestones onto the lawn.

The garden was enticing and Lila loved the pool at once. It was oval in shape and large enough to swim in. Golden fish idled between long lily stalks. A silver mermaid held a conch shell to her lips. From the shell, a fountain cascaded. The mermaid's other arm rested on a leaping dolphin, and a gleaming frog sat on the end of her fishy tail. Above, in the spray, a rainbow shimmered.

The rest of the First Years, already at the water's edge, had formed an admiring circle around Princess Bee Balm.

"This is the Bewitching Pool," she was telling them. "The statues were a present from my mother and father. They're made of silver, in keeping with the school; all the buildings here are made of silver, as you can see. And did you know that my great-great-great-grandfather founded Silverlake Fairy School here in the castle?" Her listeners shook and nodded their heads accordingly, eager for every word.

Inwardly, Lila groaned, and wondered if the Princess would spend all her time showing off. She had even attracted a group of older fairies, two of whom were particularly striking. One was a dazzling yellow, with long golden hair, and the other a midnight blue fairy with green wing tips. Both listened attentively for a few minutes before raising their eyebrows at each other and turning away. The Princess didn't notice. Lila wondered if the two fairies were thinking what she was thinking as they fluttered across the garden, deep in conversation. Mistress Pipit raised her wand and a string of tiny bells trilled for silence.

Wands and Charms

"There will be an assembly shortly, but before that I'm going to show you to your classroom. Please, follow me. Walk, no fluttering."

Chapter Three

The Hall of Rainbows

Mistress Pipit set off at a brisk pace and everyone hurried to keep up. Meggie and Lila found themselves at the front of the line.

High above them towered turret after silver turret, too many to count, but four stood out because from each pinnacle streamed a pennant; one with an orange sun, another with a moon, a third with a cloud and, furthest away of all, a glittering star. Lila pointed out the flags.

"They're beautiful," said Meggie. "I wonder what they're for."

"I hope we'll find out soon," said Lila, eager to know too.

Their teacher led them to a pair of heavy studded doors, which swung wide to allow them into a long vaulted hall. Seven gleaming chandeliers shaped like leafy branches hung from the ceiling. Each glowed a different color – red, orange, yellow, green, blue, indigo and violet. Mistress Pipit raised her wand for silence.

"Welcome to the Hall of Rainbows," she announced. "This is where we have our assemblies. Your bracelets will open the main doors for you. The rule is that you wear your bracelets at all times. Remember, if you go beyond the school walls without your bracelet, you won't be able to get back in again."

From either side of the hall, two wide staircases swept upward. A pair of flying swallows was

carved onto one staircase and two handsome owls on the other.

"The Swallow staircase and the Owl staircase," indicated Mistress Pipit.

"So-called for obvious reasons," said Princess Bee Balm, with proud assurance. Mistress Pipit turned to see who had spoken. The Princess gave her a regal smile.

"Thank you, Bee Balm. I'd prefer it if you didn't interrupt."

There was a general stir. Lila was as surprised as the rest of the class to hear the Princess being told off, especially without a "Your Majesty" or "Royal Highness." The Princess's smile vanished and she lowered her eyes, blushing, whether from embarrassment or anger Lila couldn't tell. But she made no other comment.

"The Swallow staircase is the way to the classrooms and to the rooms of magic and charms. Follow me," said Mistress Pipit, leading the way up.

The Hall of Rainbows

Meggie and Lila hurried after her.

"Excuse me, Lilac Blossom," said Princess Bee Balm. Both Lila and Meggie stopped. "I believe I go first. You have already pushed ahead of me once. Join me, Nutmeg. Be my partner."

"I already have a partner, thank you, Your Majesty," said Meggie.

"Why would you choose a kitchen fairy when you could be with me?" the Princess asked.

"Lilac Blossom is my friend," said Meggie.

A flush deepened on the Princess's cheeks. "Suit yourself!" she said and swept past, followed by her cluster of admirers. Meggie bobbed a curtsy, but Lila, distracted by a small green fairy at the back who was struggling to carry the Princess's cloak, didn't bother.

"Do you want a hand?" she asked, gathering up an armful of willow-wool. There were tears in the fairy's eyes.

"What's the matter?" Meggie asked, kindly.

The fairy was too upset to speak. She held up the edge of the white cloak. It was marked by a long green grass stain.

"I s-s-s-tepped on it by m-m-m-mistake," she stuttered, unable to hold back her sobs. Her shoulders shook.

"It was an accident," said Meggie. "The Princess will understand."

But Lila could already imagine the nasty scene that would follow when the Princess found out.

Meggie put her arm around the green fairy.

"Come on, crying isn't going to solve the problem. Dry your eyes and tell us your name." Meggie handed the fairy a yellow handkerchief.

"It's Candytuft," sobbed the fairy. "But what am I going to say? The Princess told me not to get it dirty."

"Tell her you're sorry," said Lila. "What else can you say?"

Lila and Meggie bundled Candytuft and the

The Hall of Rainbows

cloak up the stairs to the first floor, where they found two corridors, one leading to the right and the other to the left. The rest of the class had completely disappeared.

"Which way?" asked Lila. Meggie shrugged and Candytuft looked helpless. "Butterburs and bodkins," said Lila. "We're lost."

Chapter Four

Mistress Pipit— Charm One Class

"Now what do we do?" asked Meggie.

"We'll have to guess," said Lila. "I think we should try this way."

They turned right into a corridor, which glowed an inviting yellow. Almost at once a voice called after them.

"Hey, where are you three off to?"

Two tall fairies tripped after them. Lila recognized them from the garden, the dazzling yellow fairy and the midnight blue one. They were very grown-up.

"We're trying to find Mistress Pipit," said Lila.

"Then you're going the wrong way."

"Which way is it, please?" asked Meggie. "We got left behind, you see."

"We'll show you," said the yellow fairy. "We're looking out for strays like you." Lila spread her wings. "No flying," she added. "First Years aren't allowed to fly until they pass the flying test." Lila folded her wings meekly, overawed by the commanding tones.

"What flying test?" she whispered to Meggie.

"I guess we'll find out soon enough," Meggie whispered back.

"Do you think we'll have to take it today?" asked Candytuft, much too loudly for Lila and Meggie, who were on their best behavior.

"Shush!" they said together. Candytuft blew her nose on Meggie's handkerchief and sniffed.

Wands and Charms

The two fairies led them back to the staircase and into the corridor on the other side. Here the light glowed a pale orange.

"You can recognize the way by Pipity's glowtone," said the midnight blue fairy. "All the teachers mark their classroom corridors with their own special color."

"Who's Pipity?" asked Candytuft, between sniffs.

"Mistress Pipit to you," smiled the yellow fairy. "But you'll soon be calling her Pipity like the rest of us."

"You're not teachers then?" asked Lila.

The two fairies found this question funny.

"No, we're not," said the yellow fairy. "We're Fifth Years. Here you are." And, smiling broadly, the pair of them fluttered back the way they had come.

Lila, Meggie and Candytuft found themselves in front of a silver door. A windowpane glowed orange

Mistress Pipit – Charm One Class

and a sign read *Mistress Pipit – Charm One Class*.

"Candytuft, take a deep breath and stay cool," said Lila, knocking on the door.

The three of them went inside. It was an interesting classroom: round, with four arched windows high on the wall. From its circular shape, Lila guessed they must be in one of the turrets. Outside, the daylight was fading fast and the orange glow in the classroom was getting brighter by the second.

"Ah, there you are," said Mistress Pipit. "I was about to come and look for you. Find yourselves a place, please. Two minutes to settle down. Then I have some important announcements to make."

The desks were shaped like mushrooms, each with a toadstool chair. There were four free places left, one for each of them, and a spare. Candytuft sat bravely at the front, two desks away from the Princess, holding tightly to the cloak. Lila and Meggie sat side by side at the back.

Lila loved her desk and spun around on her toadstool. Meggie did the same until they were stopped by an unexpected commotion in the front row.

"Let go, you stupid fairy," ordered the Princess, wrenching her cloak from Candytuft. Unfortunately, the grass stain was discovered almost at once. "What's this?" howled Princess Bee Balm, shaking the cloak in front of Candytuft, who had covered her face with her hands. "This is willow-wool – incredibly expensive and difficult to charm. It was a present from the Lord Chamberlain. Look what you've done to it, you green goblin idiot!"

"Bee Balm!" Mistress Pipit said sharply. "That is enough."

The class froze, the only sound being Candytuft's sobs. But Princess Bee Balm was unstoppable.

"The stupid thing's got a horrid grass stain on my new cloak. I trusted her to carry it properly,

not drag it about. How can I wear it now? It's spoiled."

"Allow me," said Mistress Pipit, touching the stain with the tip of her wand. Instantly the cloak turned green. "There," she said. "The mark's invisible now."

"But I never wear green," said the Princess, aghast. "Turn it white again at once."

"As you said, my dear, willow-wool is difficult to charm. You wanted a cloak without a stain. Turning it green is the best I can do."

Lila nearly put up her hand to say that one of Cook's washing charms could get grass stains out of anything. Then thought better of it. Mistress Pipit had a look on her face that Lila found rather scary. It was a look that said she was very, very cross. Unfortunately, Princess Bee Balm didn't notice.

"And she hasn't even apologized," raged the Princess.

Mistress Pipit – Charm One Class

"Sit down, Bee Balm." Mistress Pipit's voice was icy.

The Princess plonked herself down muttering, "I never ever wear green!"

"Candytuft," said their teacher. "Come here, dear." Candytuft stood up and blew her nose into the yellow handkerchief. Mistress Pipit put a comforting arm around her shoulders.

"I'm really, really sorry. I didn't mean to st-st-step on the cloak. S-s-s-orry a th-th-th-ousand times, Your Majesty," said Candytuft, between sobs.

"Thank you, Candytuft, that was well said." Mistress Pipit turned to the Princess. "And now it's your turn to apologize, Bee Balm."

"Me! Apologize to her? What for? She's ruined my cloak!"

"It was an accident and Candytuft has said sorry. But you have used words I never again expect to hear said in my classroom by one fairy to another. That is what you must apologize for. *Do I make myself clear?*"

The Princess sat open-mouthed, while her cheeks turned from a pale pink to a deep rose. Slowly, she stood up. "Candytuft, I apologize for shouting at you and calling you names." She bobbed a curtsy to the small green fairy, then sat quickly down again.

"Thank you, Bee Balm," said Mistress Pipit. "I wish to hear no more about the incident." She gently directed Candytuft back toward her toadstool. Lila and Meggie were wide-eyed. Mistress Pipit was really strict, even with Princess Bee Balm. The teacher turned back to her class with a smile, but it took several moments for everyone to relax again.

"Very well. Now listen carefully. I have one important safety rule that must be obeyed. All First Year fairies are forbidden to fly until they pass the Flying Proficiency Test. Most of you will be able to fly quite competently, but some of you may have wings that are not yet strong enough to take you any distance. The only flying you will do, until you pass the test, will be under supervision. Is that understood?"

"Yes, Mistress Pipit." Lila and Meggie exchanged glum looks, and Lila put up her hand.

"You have a question, Lilac Blossom?"

"How long before we take the Flying Proficiency Test, please, Mistress Pipit?"

"Usually it's taken at the end of the second week of term. There'll be plenty of time to practice."

A disappointed sigh rose from the rest of the class. They must all have been thinking the same thought – two weeks on the ground was a long time!

"Don't worry, Charm One; the test will come around soon enough and with lots of practice you'll all pass first time, I'm sure." Mistress Pipit smiled fondly at her new class. "And the other thing I have to say is this: Fairy Godmother Whimbrel, our dear Headteacher, has expressly instructed that during her time here, Bee Balm, our royal Princess, is to be treated in the same way as any other pupil." Princess Bee Balm looked up in surprise. "This means that at no time in school is she to be called by any royal title, but by her name only. This may be difficult to remember at first, but I expect you to follow this instruction and make her one of us."

Bee Balm sat rigidly throughout Mistress's Pipit's speech, and Lila was certain that such a blow to her pride was not going to improve the Princess's temper.

"Now, Charm One," their teacher continued, "in a few minutes we will go down to the Hall of Rainbows for our first school assembly, where Fairy Godmother Whimbrel will welcome you to the school. During the assembly you will receive a special first charm for your Silverlake Fairy

Mistress Pipit – Charm One Class

School bracelets." A thrill of anticipation rippled among the fairies. "You will also receive a wand. Take care of it. Lost or broken wands will have to be paid for. And, finally, you will also be told which Fairy Clan you are in and you will remain in the clan throughout your time in the school. Any questions?"

A hand went up, belonging to a sea-blue fairy with violet wing tips who was sitting next to the Princess.

"Yes, Sea Holly?" said Mistress Pipit.

"If we don't like our special Fairy Charm, can we change it?"

"No, I'm afraid you can't," said Mistress Pipit. "But in my experience no fairy ever wants to change it. Are there any more questions?"

Meggie put up her hand. "Do boggarts ever get into the school? Because we're very near the Eerie Mountains," she said. There were a few gasps and shudders from the rest of the class.

Wands and Charms

"Certainly not," said Mistress Pipit. "Let me reassure you all that the school is guarded by many, many charms that keep the boggarts out, not just from the school, but also from venturing out of the mountains down to the lake. You are all quite safe here. Besides, you'll be learning the guardian charm yourselves before too long. Once you know it, no boggart will dare to come near you."

There was no time for more questions as a trill of tiny bells rang out.

"Time for assembly," said Mistress Pipit. "We'll go down to the Hall of Rainbows in orderly pairs. Find a partner, please."

A ripple of excitement spread through the class. Lila and Meggie clasped hands. For the moment the disappointment of the no-flying rule was lost at the thought of being given a wand and a special magical charm. Eyes alight, they hurried to line up. They could hardly wait.

Chapter Five

First Assembly

*C*harm One Class tripped down the Swallow staircase to find the Hall of Rainbows full of fairies. They were hovering in little groups, chattering brightly. Several were playing chase, wings sparkling like diamonds as they swooped and dived.

Lila glanced around her to see if there was another purple fairy. She saw several deep shades of violet, but nobody with the same dark hair and fingernails that she had. With so many fairies in flight, she longed to spread her wings and join them. It was an effort to keep her feet on the ground, but the no-flying rule had to be obeyed.

A few of the older fairies were already seated on toadstools at one end of the hall. At the other end was a stage with seven silver thrones in a row on it, with the grandest at the center. One or two heads turned to look with curiosity at the new Charm One Class as Mistress Pipit led the way forward. The chattering gradually faded and, as if by an invisible signal, all the fairies fluttered to their places.

Six teachers appeared on the stage. Quite where they came from, Lila couldn't tell, but Mistress Pipit joined them and all the pupils stood and curtsied politely.

The older fairy, in front of the grandest throne, rested a hand firmly on the lid of a silver chest that sat by her on a small table. From inside the chest came the sound of tapping, as if a thousand raindrops were eager to be let out. Lila was intrigued by the chest but was even more curious about the fairy. Dressed in an elegant purple and silver gown, she wore a pair of spectacles on the end of her nose. But most exciting of all, her elegantly pointed wings were veined dark purple and her sparkling fingernails were an identical color to Lila's. The one obvious difference between their colorings was the silver-gray streak in the fairy's purple hair. Lila nudged Meggie and beamed happily. This was the first time she had seen another fairy the same color as herself.

Applause started at the back of the hall and soon the whole school was clapping an enthusiastic welcome to their teachers. The chandeliers puffed out rainbow clouds, each floating across the ceiling before dissolving with a pop. The purple fairy smiled and, when it seemed the applause would go on forever, raised her hand. A bracelet, heavy with charms, slid up her arm, tinkling merrily.

First Assembly

"A warm welcome to you all and especially to the new First Years," she said. Mistress Pipit's class curtsied low at the honor and everyone sat down. "Allow me to introduce myself to our new Charm One pupils. My name is Fairy Godmother Whimbrel and I am your Headteacher."

Lila couldn't have been more delighted. To be the identical color to someone as important as that was the nicest surprise.

"Charm Five," said Fairy Godmother Whimbrel, addressing the most grown-up fairies at the back of the hall. "It's good to see you so cheerful, and ready for your final year as top class. I know you'll be an inspiration to all the other pupils in the school." She smiled. "And now the news you've all been waiting to hear. It gives me great pleasure to announce that this year's Head Fairy is Day Lily."

The yellow fairy that Lila and Meggie had already met flew to the stage and, amid the loud cheers of her classmates, she curtsied.

"Wow," said Meggie. "We've met her."

"And we know she's really nice," smiled Lila.

"Congratulations, Day Lily," smiled Godmother Whimbrel. "Day Lily's deputy will be Musk Mallow." This was the midnight blue fairy whom they had also met. There were more cheers as Musk Mallow took her place next to Day Lily. They gave each other a hug. Lila and Meggie clapped until their hands tingled.

By this time, another of the teachers had both hands on the lid of the silver chest and could barely keep it on the table.

"We'd better begin, dears," said Godmother Whimbrel, raising her wand. A whirlwind of green and silver stars cascaded onto the stage in front of her and made a perfect fairy ring. It was edged with delicate toadstools and the grass in the center was a lush green.

Meggie and Lila glanced at each other, wondering what was going to happen next. Day Lily and

First Assembly

Musk Mallow placed the table with the silver chest next to the fairy ring.

"Now, Charm One, you are each going to receive your first *special* fairy charm," said Godmother Whimbrel. "This charm chooses you. But, if you work hard during your first year, you will earn three more charms, one at the end of each term. To do that you must pass your charm exams. Then, at the end of the school year, you'll be ready to move up to Charm Two. If you fail to earn those three important charms this school year, you will stay in Charm One Class until you do. But I'm sure you will all work hard. Indeed, I expect no less. And hard work will bring success."

Lila wondered what her *special* charm would be. It sounded so exciting.

"You will also receive a school wand. It will have a sun, moon, cloud or star at its tip. This will indicate the Fairy Clan to which you will belong.

Wands and Charms

I am in the Star Clan and Mistress Pipit is in the Sun Clan." She turned to the Charm One Class teacher. "Please will you start us off?"

Mistress Pipit walked to the center of the stage and consulted the list on her scroll. There was a pause, and the whole class leaned forward, expectantly. Lila's heart began to race. Who would be chosen to go first?

Chapter Six

Charms and Clans

"Candytuft," announced Mistress Pipit.

There was a disappointed sigh from the rest of the class, who would now have to wait. "Come onto the stage." Candytuft rose uncertainly to her feet. The Princess was frowning. For once, Lila could understand Bee Balm's frustration, for although she hadn't expected to go first, she would have liked to. Day Lily took Candytuft by the hand and led her into the fairy ring.

"There's nothing to worry about, Candytuft,

dear," said Fairy Godmother Whimbrel. "All you have to do is stand quietly. Ready?" Candytuft nodded and Musk Mallow released the catch on the chest.

The lid burst open in a glittering explosion. Silver charms flew into the fairy ring and spun around and around, weaving Candytuft into a thousand threads of brilliant light. Then, as dramatically as they had arrived, they dived back into the chest and Musk Mallow shut the lid. Lila turned astonished eyes to Meggie.

"There are hundreds and hundreds of them," she whispered.

"Look," said Meggie. "Look!" A tiny silver frog dangled from Candytuft's bracelet. "What will choose us, Lila? What will it be?"

Candytuft gazed in wonder at the little frog.

"Now, Candytuft, stay in the fairy ring. I'm going to give you a wand. Are you ready?" Again, Candytuft nodded.

Charms and Clans

Fairy Godmother Whimbrel stepped into the fairy ring and with the lightest touch of her wand brushed Candytuft's pale hair with the star at its tip. There was a puff of rainbow stardust and Candytuft found herself holding a green wand with a little cloud on the end. "As you see, my dear, you will be in the Cloud Clan. Use your wand and charm well. I'm sure you'll find a good use for that little frog."

"Thank you, Fairy Godmother," said Candytuft, with a shy curtsy. Both fairies stepped out of the ring, and Candytuft went back to her place, showing the wand and charm to everyone who wanted to look.

Two more fairies were called to receive their charms and wands. Then Mistress Pipit called out Nutmeg's name.

"Good luck," whispered Lila.

Meggie stepped into the fairy ring, fixing her eyes on the silver chest. Up went the lid and out came the charms. They spun around her far longer than they had with the other three fairies, making a cloud so thick that Meggie was lost from view. It was as if the charms couldn't decide which should go to her. But at last they went back into the chest, leaving behind a delicate pair of silver scissors hanging on the bracelet.

"I wonder what you'll be cutting out with those," said Godmother Whimbrel as she joined Meggie in the fairy ring.

"Gossamer fabric, if I'm lucky," smiled Meggie. "I love making things." A puff of rainbow stardust left Meggie holding a delicate golden yellow wand tipped with a star.

"Use your charm and wand well, my dear. You join the Star Clan."

"It's easy-peasy," Meggie whispered to Lila as she took her seat again. "And I love my little scissors."

"Maybe you can turn them into a real pair with your wand," Lila whispered back.

Charms and Clans

"Maybe!" said Meggie. "I wonder if I can?"

Fairy after fairy came and went. All kinds of different charms were given out, from spoons to rabbits, from songbirds to flowers, and each fairy appeared pleased with the charm she received. The last two left to go were Bee Balm and Lila. By this time there was barely any noise coming from the chest. It was as if the charms knew there were only two more to be given out.

Bee Balm's name was called next. With a look at Lila which said, *At least I get to go before you,* the Princess rose gracefully, shook the crumples from her dress and took her place in the fairy ring. There was a stir from the rest of the school.

"Everyone knows who she is," whispered Meggie.

"And everyone thinks she's beautiful and nice," whispered back Lila.

"Not everyone," said Meggie.

From out of the silver chest came a single charm.

It flew purposefully toward the Princess. A few others tried to follow but the lone charm drove the stragglers back. There was no clamor or competition for Princess Bee Balm. The one charm flew to her bracelet and that was that.

"A dog," exclaimed Meggie, surprised.

"A fox," announced Bee Balm. "A beautiful silver fox!" There was silence in the hall, and Lila wondered why only the one charm had been so determined to reach the Princess's bracelet. It must have been that the fox charm was so fierce that none of the other charms dared challenge it. She gave a little shiver. Bee Balm stood serenely before Fairy Godmother Whimbrel and received an elegant pink wand with a sun at its tip.

"You are in the Sun Clan, as you see. Use your wand and charm well," said Fairy Godmother Whimbrel. "The intelligence and cunning of the fox can be used for bad as well as good. Please remember that."

Charms and Clans

"Of course I will," said Bee Balm, curtsying deeply. She went back to her place, stroking her silver charm as if in a dream.

"And finally, Lilac Blossom," announced Mistress Pipit.

"Good luck," Meggie whispered.

Lila rose to her feet. It had been a long wait and part of her felt disappointed that so few charms were coming out of the chest now. She couldn't bring herself to look into the sea of fairy faces in the hall; there were so many of them, and, scarily, they were all looking at her. She stood nervously in the fairy ring, the grass springy under her feet, and fastened her attention on the chest. A sudden commotion inside, more violent than any before, set her heart pounding. Fairy Godmother Whimbrel gazed calmly toward her and their eyes met. At once, Lila felt reassured and ready for anything.

The lid burst open and a thick swarm of charms sped toward her. They spun silver streamers

around her, blotting out everything else. Clusters of charms approached and receded. A sudden dizziness made Lila close her eyes. When she opened them again the charms were gone. She held up her bracelet.

"I've got a unicorn!" she said, wonder in her voice. The tiny unicorn glittered silver and purple. Lila couldn't take her eyes from him, hardly aware of the applause ringing in her ears. She remembered her swim in the river a few days before the Silverlake Fairy School entrance test. A unicorn had watched her come out of the water. His coat had been silver-white, but his mane and tail were purple. He was the most magical of creatures. The charm on her bracelet felt just right.

"Remember, Lilac Blossom, a unicorn is a rare and powerful charm," said Fairy Godmother Whimbrel, stepping into the fairy ring and looking down at her. "With power comes responsibility. Use him wisely."

Lila looked up at the Headteacher. "But how?"

"I can't tell you that. Each charm is as unique as you are. It's a mystery for you to work out."

The fairy godmother touched Lila's hair lightly with her wand.

"My dear, you join the Star Clan," she smiled.

Somehow Lila found a purple wand in her hand. The star at its tip showed just what she had wished for – to be in the same Fairy Clan as Meggie. Her work done, Fairy Godmother Whimbrel slipped her own wand back into her sleeve and the fairy ring vanished. Lila curtsied and met Bee Balm's envious stare. The Princess lowered her eyes at once, but Lila knew that somehow she had overshadowed the beautiful pink fairy. Applause still echoed in her ears. But what had she done to deserve it?

Meggie pulled Lila into her place and hugged her.

"There," she told Lila. "It may be rare to be

purple, but it seems to be seriously special. A unicorn chose you."

"Yes," said Lila dreamily. "A silver unicorn!" She would take the greatest care of him and one day, if she was very clever, she might make him come alive.

Chapter Seven

First Day Feast

"Stars to me. This way, all First Year Stars!"

After the charm-giving, the end of assembly came quickly in a great hustle and bustle. Charm One had been instructed to find their clan leaders. Lila and Meggie held tight to one another as fairies hurried in all directions.

"Moons over here. All Charm One Moons this way."

Each First Year hurried to find out where they had to be.

First Day Feast

"Suns, come to me, please. I said Suns. You're a Cloud. You go over there."

It was confusing for the new Charm One Class, as other fairies hailed each other and met up and flew away again in a flurry of sparkling wings.

"Stars this way. Over here, all Stars."

Lila and Meggie found it was Musk Mallow calling for the Stars. Not only was she Deputy Head Fairy, she was also Head of the Star Clan as well.

"Welcome, Stars," said Musk Mallow, counting six of them, including a woebegone sky-blue fairy Lila hadn't noticed before. Musk Mallow winked at the fairy as if she already knew her. The fairy frowned and studied her toes. "Attention, everyone, it's time for the First Day feast. You must be starving, all of you, after your long journey here. I know I am. I'm going to take you to the refectory now. All meals are served there. After the feast it'll be bedtime and I'll take you to the Star Clan dormitory."

Wands and Charms

They followed Musk Mallow up the Owl staircase. Other Heads of Clan fairies were leading their First Years in the same direction. There was quite a crowd and Lila accidentally stepped on the pink hem of the fairy in front of her. Unfortunately, it belonged to Bee Balm. She turned and glared.

"Sorry, Your Highness," said Lila, adding the royal title before she could stop herself.

"Stupid kitchen fairy! Trust you," Bee Balm said, and turned away with a flounce.

"Wow, whatever did you do to her?" asked the sky-blue fairy, stepping up beside Lila.

"I wish I knew," said Lila, with a grimace. "Are you a First Year too? You weren't in the classroom earlier."

"Failed all last year's charm exams," said the sky-blue fairy, with a sigh.

Princess Bee Balm glanced around to see who was speaking, before hurrying on ahead.

"I've got the world's worst memory. I'll probably

be in Charm One for the rest of my life. But at least I've got this." And she held out her school bracelet to show Lila and Meggie her special charm – a little silver hat.

"That is elegant," said Meggie. "Look, it's decorated with a feather."

"And I have my Flying Proficiency Certificate," the fairy added.

"Your memory can't be that bad," said Lila. "You remembered enough to pass the school entrance test."

"That was because my ogre of an aunt made me practice entrance tests every day for a year," said the fairy and grinned. "It was impossible not to remember something."

"I'm Lilac Blossom," said Lila, liking the fairy at once. "And this is Nutmeg."

"Hello," said the sky-blue fairy. "I'm Harebell, but my friends call me Bella."

"Mine call me Lila, and this is Meggie," said Lila.

Bella's grin grew broader. "Since I've done everything once, second time around should be easier," she reasoned.

"And you'll be able to help us when we get stuck," said Meggie.

"Um...possibly," said Bella. "Chances are it'll be you helping me."

"We can all help each other," said Lila, and the three fairies linked arms in happy agreement.

The refectory was at the top of the stairs and, as they turned toward it, the air became filled with delicious smells.

"I'm starving," said Lila.

"Me too," Meggie and Bella chorused.

They followed Musk Mallow through the refectory door into a huge room with six giant mushroom tables in it. Several teachers were already seated on cushioned toadstools.

"As you can see," said Musk Mallow, pointing, "the mistresses sit at the top table. This is the

First Day Feast

First Year table. You've got Bella here to tell you what's what. I'll catch up with you later." And, with a smile, Musk Mallow fluttered off to join the Fifth Years.

As soon as everyone had found a place, Fairy Godmother Whimbrel stood up and a hush fell.

"Now we are all gathered together, I wish you a delicious First Day feast. May this be the start of a productive year for you all. But before we begin, I'd like to thank our cook, Fairy Flowerdew, for the delicious treats that are to come. I know she's been very busy in the kitchen." A red-faced fairy wearing a large white apron appeared by the mistresses's table.

"That's her," said Bella. "I wonder what she's charmed for us this feast."

Fairy Flowerdew curtsied and raised her wand, filling the refectory with a burst of red and silver stardust. From inside the shimmering cloud, all manner of platters and bowls drifted down onto the tables. There were dandelion fritters and crystallized thistledown. There was a great bowl of frosted dill-leaf salad; another of plovers' eggs in aspic. Lila spotted the biggest pile ever of rosemary crunch. There were honeysuckle-and-nut burgers and pomegranate relish. There was the most enormous wobbly, blackcurrant and spice jelly and a great bowl of saffron cream. There were nut-and-ginger cookies and chocolate fudge seedcake. There were jugs of honey-and-fruit punch. Lila was overwhelmed. This was the sort of feast that Cook charmed for Their Royal Majesties.

"Help yourselves, everybody," said Bella, reaching for the dandelion fritters before anyone else could get them. "It doesn't get this good again until the end of the school year."

"Don't grab," said Bee Balm, smacking Bella's arm with her wand. "Don't you have any manners? Candytuft, you may serve me. I would like a little of everything except the plover eggs."

First Day Feast

Candytuft's face fell at being singled out again, but she stood up to do as she was told.

"It's all right, Candytuft, you don't have to take orders from Bee Balm," said Lila.

"Oh, doesn't she?" said Bee Balm. "After what she did to my cloak I think serving me is the least she can do."

"It was an accident. You know that."

"If she's not going to serve me, then you can," said Bee Balm, thrusting her plate at Lila. "After all, you're a kitchen fairy. You should be good at it."

"Maybe I am," said Lila. "But nobody should have to serve anybody else. We're all equal here. You heard what Mistress Pipit said."

There was an awkward silence. None of the First Years moved. Bee Balm glared at Lila and Lila glared stubbornly back. The stalemate was broken by Musk Mallow coming to check on them. She raised an eyebrow at the reluctant diners.

"What's up with you all? Come on, everybody, help yourselves. You start, Bee Balm. You must be used to feasts, living in the Royal Palace."

Bee Balm tossed her head, smiled and, probably for the first time in her life, lifted a serving spoon and put food on her plate. She did it without showing a flicker of annoyance, as though she had intended to do that all along. But Lila wasn't fooled for a moment. Soon the whole table was eating and enjoying the delicious food as though nothing had happened, and Bee Balm was chatting away to the blue fairy next to her, who Lila remembered, was called Sea Holly. Satisfied all was well, Musk Mallow went back to her place.

Lila did her best to enjoy the feast, but was waiting to see what would happen next, certain that Bee Balm wouldn't let things rest. She didn't have to wait long. As soon as Bee Balm finished eating, she thoughtfully licked a chocolatey finger.

Wands and Charms

"I think we should try out our charms," she said. "They must do something. Harebell, what's yours? Even if you have failed your First Year, you must know how to work your special charm."

Bella, who was about to take a bite from a piece of rosemary crunch, turned suspicious eyes toward the Princess.

Bee Balm smiled sweetly and encouragingly. "Or are you really as stupid as failing all your exams makes you seem?"

Lila flinched on her friend's behalf, but Bella put a hand on Lila's arm to keep her silent.

"I only talk about my charm with my friends," Bella said.

"Well, come on then," said Bee Balm, with a smile.

"I said I only talk about my—"

"I heard what you said. I thought you might like to be my friend?"

"Whatever made you think that?"

First Day Feast

There were surprised gasps from several of the watching fairies. Bella took a big bite from her piece of crunch. Still chewing, she picked up a plate and offered it to Lila and Meggie. "This is great. Want some?" Bella's meaning could not have been plainer. She had chosen her friends. Lila and Meggie both took a piece of crunch and bit into it.

Bee Balm ignored the slight and, with a tinkling laugh, carried on. "I think a charm probably works like a dream wish. We did one of those for the school entrance test, remember, everyone? Lilac Blossom was incredibly good at it." She gave Lila a sweet smile as if to remind her. "We'll all try. I really want my fox to come alive. Come on, everybody, get out your wands." And she lifted her pink wand, shut her eyes and tapped the silver fox charm. The table waited agog, but nothing happened. "Oh, no," said the Princess, as if she hadn't expected it to. "I don't seem to be able to do it. Lilac Blossom, if you would be so good? Dream wish my fox for me."

"He's your charm, not mine," Lila said.

"She's right," added Bella. "You're supposed to work out your own charm, not get somebody else to do it for you. I'm still working on mine."

"Yes, well, you would be," said Bee Balm.

"It's not just me," said Bella. "Lots of fairies all the way up the school have never made their charms do anything."

"Well, I'm not waiting. I want Lilac Blossom to dream wish my fox tonight. It's a royal command."

"I'm not going to. It would be stupid to try," said Lila.

"Are you calling me stupid?" Bee Balm's eyes flashed.

"No," said Lila.

"Don't you mean, 'No, Your Majesty'?"

Mistress Pipit had told them they were not to

call the Princess by any royal title and Lila was not going to give in.

"No, Bee Balm."

The Princess trilled with merriment. Several other fairies joined in, but there was a brittle edge to the laughter and Lila knew the Princess was furious.

"It was a fine feast, wasn't it?" said Bee Balm, turning to Candytuft.

"Yes, Your Majesty," said Candytuft.

"Did you manage a dream wish at the test? I didn't. I simply can't do them. I bet you did one, didn't you?"

"Only a little one," said Candytuft, modestly. The Princess smiled and raised an eyebrow. Candytuft realized too late what she was about to be asked. "Oh, no, no, I don't want to do it."

"You know, it's a funny thing, but I was only asking the Lord Chamberlain before I left what would happen to anyone who damaged my new cloak, seeing as it was such an expensive and special present. And do you know what he said?" The Princess paused for effect. "He said they would be banished from the Kingdom."

Candytuft's face crumpled.

"You w-w-wouldn't tell him, would you? Please, don't," she pleaded.

"I might have to."

Lila's spirits sank. It was a well-known fact at the palace that the Lord Chamberlain doted on Bee Balm. He and the Princess were always hatching plans together. Could he have said such a thing? Would Bee Balm really tell him about the cloak? Lila took a deep breath.

"I'll dream wish your fox if you're sure that's what you want." She knew it was a bad idea, but she had to help Candytuft. Lila took out her wand.

"Don't do it," whispered Bella. "It could mean big trouble."

First Day Feast

But Lila couldn't bear to see Candytuft that deathly white and scared. It was worth a try. If she succeeded, maybe Bee Balm would be satisfied. Of course, this was very different than the dream wish she had done in the test. That had come out of her imagination. The silver fox was a real charm. She didn't know how to do it and had no idea what might happen if the dream wish actually worked.

Bella put her hands over her ears and scrunched up her face as though expecting something cataclysmic. Lila tapped the silver fox with the tip of her wand. In her mind she recalled the handsome fox that she had sometimes seen patrolling the courtyard at the Fairy Palace. Lila often left out scraps for him secretly. Cook would have been furious if she'd known. She shut her eyes tight to think harder. He came in the night, walking in the shadows, but once or twice she had caught him standing in the pool of light from the window. His coat was silver and gray, except his underbelly, which was white. He had black ear tips and legs, and a bushy tail with a white tip. His dark eyes gleamed. He could leap and bounce and vanish like a ghost.

Lila heard the fairies around her gasp and she opened her eyes. The entire Charm One Class table was staring nervously at a large fox standing among the empty platters. He looked around, then dropped his head to lick the Princess's plate with a long pink tongue.

When the plate was clean he looked directly at Lila and appeared to grin. Lila felt incredibly proud of herself.

Bee Balm stroked the fox's furry back. He writhed away from the touch and a low rumble came from his throat; his upper lip curled, revealing two rows of sharp white teeth and his eyes narrowed with hostility. Bee Balm snatched her hand away. The fox wasn't the loveable creature she had expected. Lila's jaw dropped. The silver fox charm still dangled from the Princess's bracelet. Surely that wasn't right?

"I told you not to do it," said Bella. "This is trouble with a capital 'T'."

Chapter Eight

Dream Wish Horror

Bee Balm staggered back from the table and Lila knew at once that she had made a terrible mistake. The fox gave Lila another of his grins, bared his teeth at the Princess and moved toward her. Bee Balm shrieked and fled out of the door. The fox bounded after her, his bushy tail floating behind him, and in a second he too was gone.

"If it *is* Bee Balm's fox," said Lila, "why is the charm still on her bracelet?"

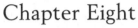 "Because the charm hasn't come alive," cried

Dream Wish Horror

Bella. "The fox is pure dream wish. Your dream wish, Lila! You've got to stop it."

"Yes," said Meggie, grabbing Lila's arm, as everyone in Charm One began to panic. "And quickly, before something dreadful happens."

"But how?"

"I don't know!" Bella said, pushing the dazed Lila toward the door. "But that fox looked hungry enough to eat a dozen Princesses. You've got to try."

"Eat her?" Lila was appalled. What had started out as the best day of her life was turning into the worst.

By now the commotion had attracted the attention of the rest of the diners. Day Lily and Musk Mallow were on their way to find out what was going on and all the teachers were looking toward the Charm One Class table.

Before anyone could stop her, Lila ran. From the top of the stairs she saw the fox cantering down after Bee Balm, who was at the great doors.

"Fly!" yelled Lila, but the panicked Princess squeezed through the gap, leaving the safety of the Hall of Rainbows, and darted into the night. The fox slipped between the doors and vanished after her.

Lila had to catch up fast. A unicorn would gallop faster than the wind. If only she could summon the silver one from her bracelet. There was no time to try. Lila jumped into the air and flew down the stairs. Now *she* had broken the no-flying rule. More trouble!

Outside, a full moon had turned the garden a silver-yellow. After the brilliance of the Hall of Rainbows, Lila's eyes took a moment to adjust. She hovered above the lawn, peering this way and that, until she saw the fox slipping through the shadows toward the silver-pink figure of the Princess crouching at the edge of the Bewitching Pool.

"He's behind you," Lila shouted. "Fly!"

Dream Wish Horror

The Princess gave a cry and fell backward into the water. Lila swooped down, pointing her wand at the fox. Purple stars whooshed toward him, although why or how she had no idea. The fox didn't like them. He flattened his ears and scampered out of the way. Then he looked to see if the stars were gone and, with a sniff, bounded down the bank into the pool.

"He can swim!" groaned Lila. "Now what should I do?" And then it came to her. Dream wish the fox into something else. Why hadn't she thought of that before?

She landed on the grass and did her best to imagine the fox with a scaly fish tail and big, round, watery eyes. But it was hard to concentrate The Princess was trying to climb onto the mermaid fountain but kept slipping back into the water. The fox was swimming steadily across the pool and had almost reached his prey. Lila took to the air again. The Princess, in a panic, half fluttered up, half climbed the mermaid at last.

"It's going to get me," she screeched.

Lila hovered, shooting more stars from her wand. The fox bobbed underwater to avoid them. Where was he? The Princess had reached the mermaid's shoulders and was now half hidden under an umbrella of water.

"I can't hang on for long," she shouted. "It's slippery."

A crowd of fairies spilled out of the Hall of Rainbows and fluttered across the moonlit grass, Bella and Meggie leading the way. Lila landed on the bank and ran around the pool. The fox had to surface soon.

"There he is," shouted Bella. "Over there."

Lila flew low and hid behind the dolphin. She could see the fox now on the far side of the mermaid. She waited. He put a paw over the mermaid's tail. This was her best chance so far. She closed her eyes and concentrated on turning

the fox's brush into a fish's tail. She gave him round, gentle eyes and in her mind his fur dissolved into golden scales while his legs became fins and his ears smoothed into a rounded head. His teeth became a gaping mouth. She opened her eyes to see what effect this imagining might have had.

"Do something," shouted Bee Balm. "I can't hang on any longer."

The words were no sooner out than she began to slip; down the Princess came, gathering speed, sliding fast along the mermaid's tail before ending up in the water with a splash. The fox sprang and Lila darted, wand outstretched. It touched his nose. There was an immediate transformation. Half fox, with a fish's tail, he spun in the air and dived. By the time he hit the water he was all fish, his golden scales reflecting moonlight.

"Thank goodness," said Lila, trembling with relief. "Bee Balm, are you all right?"

Dream Wish Horror

"Where is it?" screeched the Princess.

"It's a goldfish now. I don't think they bite."

Lila offered the Princess her hand, but it was pushed aside and Bee Balm clambered out by herself. Fairy Godmother Whimbrel and Mistress Pipit were waiting for them on the grass, with what appeared to be the whole school behind them. Lila saw Meggie's anxious face in the crowd, and Bella gave her a thumbs-up sign.

"I'm sorry," she apologized. "It was all a terrible mistake." Princess Bee Balm said nothing. Her beautiful pink dress was covered with green pond weed, her pink tresses stuck to her head and pond water, or maybe it was tears, ran in rivulets down her cheeks "And I'm afraid I've broken my wand," Lila added, noticing that the star on the end was hanging by a miserable thread.

Was this to be the end of her Silverlake Fairy School career, over before it had really begun? Whatever was she going to tell Cook? Lila looked up at Fairy Godmother Whimbrel, expecting to be expelled on the spot, and blinked back her own tears.

Chapter Nine

Is This The End?

Nothing was said. Instead Fairy Godmother Whimbrel rested her wand on Lila's shoulder and Mistress Pipit did the same with the Princess. At once, they were surrounded by swirling stars and a furious wind that lifted them up and carried them off.

As quickly as it had come, the wind died away and Lila found herself standing next to Bee Balm in a circular room, smaller than the classroom, and made cozy by a log fire that blazed in a wide grate.

Wands and Charms

Fairy Godmother Whimbrel sat behind an oak desk with several parchments on it. The silver charms chest was sitting calmly on the mantelpiece above the fire. The Headteacher slipped her wand into her sleeve, not for one second taking her eyes from Lila and Bee Balm. Mistress Pipit remained at her side, arms folded and with a stern expression on her face.

Lila glimpsed Bee Balm's defiant stare before looking down at the carpet. Would she get sent straight home, she wondered, and was it possible that the Princess might be expelled too? The fire crackled and spat. At last Fairy Godmother Whimbrel broke the silence.

"I am astonished by what has gone on this evening, and on your first day at school; such extraordinary, wild behavior from you both. I would like an explanation, please." There was a pause while Lila waited to see if the Princess would speak.

Is This The End?

"I'm truly sorry," Lila said into the silence. "I flew because I wanted to stop the fox. It was the fastest way to help Her Royal— I mean, Bee Balm. She was in great danger, you see. I know I've let you down. I didn't mean to. I should never have done the dream wish in the first place."

"The fox was your dream wish, was it?" asked Fairy Godmother Whimbrel, exchanging a glance with Mistress Pipit. Lila nodded miserably, a lump choking her throat.

"It was supposed to bring Princess Bee Balm's fox charm to life, but it didn't work. The charm never left her bracelet."

The Princess glanced around and from her surprised expression Lila realized she hadn't known that.

"And whose idea was this daring experiment?"

This was definitely the Princess's cue to say something but she continued to stare ahead, and Lila couldn't bring herself to tell tales. It was a relief when Fairy Godmother Whimbrel turned away.

"Lilac Blossom appears to be speechless. Perhaps, Bee Balm, you can explain your part in this unfortunate episode?"

"Oh, but it's obvious. I was forced to escape from the terrifying creature she created," said Bee Balm. "It meant to kill me. Did you see its teeth?" Bee Balm turned to Lila with an angry flounce. "You'd have enjoyed seeing me torn to shreds, wouldn't you?"

"I didn't know the fox would chase you," said Lila. "You should have thought of the danger before you asked me to dream wish your charm."

"Asked you!" said Bee Balm. "It was your idea. I would never have thought of anything so stupid. She begged me to let her. She went on and on, 'Let me dream wish your charm, please, let me,' so naturally in the end I gave in."

"That's not true," Lila objected.

Is This The End?

"See how she lies," the Princess continued. "But what can you expect from a kitchen fairy? She's only a servant. She should never have been accepted at a school like this. I told my parents—"

"Bee Balm! You have said quite enough!" said Godmother Whimbrel, bringing the Princess to an abrupt stop.

Lila's pale skin flushed a dark purple and her temples throbbed. She didn't dare look at either of the mistresses. Now they knew exactly what the Princess thought of her. Then, taking courage, she looked directly at the Headteacher and said, "I am not a liar. Everything I've said has been the truth. I may be a kitchen fairy, but at least I know I'm honest."

"Well," said Fairy Godmother Whimbrel. "I have two different versions of events. Which one of you am I to believe?"

"You could ask the other First Years," said Lila. "Lots of them saw what happened."

The Princess looked startled. Clearly she hadn't thought of that. Now it was her turn to blush.

"Yes, indeed, we could do that," said Godmother Whimbrel. "But I don't think it will be necessary, will it, Bee Balm?"

The Princess tossed her head as if nothing she had said before really mattered. "Very well, I did command Lila to do the dream wish. She can do them and I can't." Then, she added in a wheedling tone, caressing her charm, "I wanted to see my little silver foxy come alive." It was the sort of voice she used with the Lord Chamberlain. It made no impression at all on the Headteacher.

"Lilac Blossom, you do know that dream wishing a wild animal like a fox was a very foolish thing to try?" said Fairy Godmother Whimbrel.

Lila nodded. "I suppose I should have realized. I didn't want to do it."

"Then why did you?"

"Because, well, because…" Lila faltered.

Is This The End?

"Very well, Bee Balm, the truth, please."

"Oh all right. I may have said something about telling the Lord Chamberlain about Candytuft's accident with my cloak."

"Yes?"

"And perhaps I did mention that she might be banished."

"I see!"

"I wasn't actually going to tell him. It was a sort of joke."

"And when things didn't turn out as you would have liked, you blamed Lilac Blossom."

"No! Well, I suppose so," said the Princess.

"There is no *suppose* about it. Yet, on the other hand, Lilac Blossom, seeing what she had done, did her best to save you from the fox and broke the no-flying rule to do it, putting her school career in jeopardy. You were lucky not to have been bitten. I hope you will both learn from this incident." Fairy Godmother Whimbrel sat back, allowing her words to sink in. After a painful silence, she turned to her fellow teacher. "What will we do with them, Mistress Pipit?"

"I suggest that Bee Balm be sent to the kitchen to work there until the morning," said their teacher. "There are plenty of dishes to do after the feast. I think she needs to learn how important the kitchen fairies are to the smooth running of our school, just as they are to the Royal Palace. I'm sure the staff will be delighted to have the extra help."

Bee Balm covered up her dismay with a blank stare. Lila knew what it hid. If the Princess had disliked her before, they had become real enemies now.

"Very well," said Fairy Godmother Whimbrel. "I agree."

Mistress Pipit rested her wand on the Princess's shoulder and they vanished into a brilliant orange sunbeam.

"And what will I do with you, Lilac Blossom?"

Is This The End?

Lila felt wretched, waiting for the verdict on her own conduct. Fairy Godmother Whimbrel sat back in her chair.

"I'm not surprised to see that you're upset," she said kindly. "The trouble you're in came from a desire to help another. I should explain that the dream wish didn't break a school rule, although, as I said, they should be used with caution. But, alas, the flying did. You had good reason for breaking the rule, I understand that. If you had not flown, you would not have reached the fox in time to change the dream wish, and then what might have happened to our dear Princess?"

Lila felt even more wretched. With a trembling hand she placed her broken wand on the desk and the star finally fell off.

"I'm afraid I don't have any money for a new one," she said.

"Ah, the broken wand, dear me," said Fairy

Is This The End?

Godmother Whimbrel. "I had forgotten about that."

"But when I get back to the palace I will ask Cook to pay for it."

"No, dear, you'll need a new wand long before the end of term."

Lila looked up. "You mean I'm not going to be expelled?"

"Goodness me, no! Punished, yes, for breaking the no-flying rule. You will spend your free time tomorrow polishing the mermaid in the Bewitching Pool. She's covered in mud and pond weed and looks disgusting."

"Don't worry, I'll make her nice and clean," promised Lila. Polishing was easy. She had been polishing all her life. "Thank you, thank you for not sending me away."

"I had no intention of sending you anywhere," Fairy Godmother Whimbrel said, fumbling in her sleeve for her wand. As she did so, Lila saw a unicorn among the many charms on her bracelet. "And remember this: Princess Bee Balm is not as powerful as she would like to think." There was a puff of silver dust. "Take it," the Headteacher said, holding out Lila's wand, mended and as good as new. "Wands are delicate. Treat it more carefully in the future."

"Yes, Godmother Whimbrel, thank you," said Lila. She took a deep breath. "May I...?" But her courage failed her and she couldn't get the words out.

"Yes?" said the Fairy Godmother, looking expectantly over the top of her spectacles.

Lila cleared her throat. "May I see your unicorn charm?"

The Headteacher's expression became unfathomable. Was she cross? Was she amused? Lila bit her lip.

"You have sharp eyes, Lilac Blossom," she said at last. "I do believe my unicorn charm is similar to the one you received today. Show me." Lila held out her bracelet. "Yes, similar but not identical. As I told you, each charm is unique." Fairy Godmother Whimbrel slid her bracelet down her wrist and picked out the unicorn. "His name is Pelorus. Now that *might* be a clue as to how you can summon your unicorn."

"Is it?" asked Lila. "Oh, you mean if I found out his name he might come alive! I hope I can. I will try, really try."

"I'm sure you will," said Fairy Godmother Whimbrel. "But it's late. Way past your bedtime and you've got a lot to do tomorrow."

"Yes," said Lila. "I'll polish the mermaid until she gleams."

"I expect nothing less," said the Headteacher. "And no more breaking school rules. They are there for a purpose. Goodnight, Lilac Blossom."

She stretched across the desk and touched Lila's shoulder with her wand. Lila was gone before she had time to say another word. This time she traveled alone with the stars and wind and they left her in a bedroom where moonlight flooded through a high window onto three beds. Two of the beds were occupied. As Lila listened she could hear the regular breathing of sleeping fairies. She crept over to see who they were. One was Meggie and the other Bella. Lila smiled with happiness. What a lot she had to tell them in the morning! And tomorrow she would begin her letter to Mip and one to Cook. She felt a little pang of homesickness and shivered.

Her trunk was waiting next to the empty bed and someone had thoughtfully unpacked her nightdress and laid it out ready. She slipped out of her gossamer frock and put it on. It was a wonderful feeling to slide under the covers, where it was warm and cozy, and snuggle down. She yawned, then held her charm to her lips and gave her unicorn a little kiss.

Is This The End?

"What are you called?" she whispered. "I hope I find out soon." Holding him to her cheek she tried to guess, but before she could think of a single name, she fell fast asleep.

Silverlake
Fairy School

For a taste of Lila's next
fairy school adventure, read...

Ready to Fly

The bells trilled for the end of break and Lila, Meggie and Bella gathered with the rest of Charm One Class beside the Bewitching Pool. Mistress Pipit arrived and held up her hand for silence.

"Now I hope you're feeling inspired after having seen your first Bugs and Butterflies game because it's time for us, as a class, to get down to some serious work." She paused and smiled. "You've done very well in our fairy gym lessons in the garden. I think you're ready for the next step. Today, you're going to have your first flying lesson in the Flutter Tower."

"We're going to fly," cried Lila, jumping up and down. "At last, at last, at last!" Mistress Pipit gave Lila one of her quelling looks and Princess Bee Balm gave a haughty sniff in her direction, but Lila was too excited to care. From her bedroom window in the Star Clan turret, she had often looked at the Flutter Tower, standing higher than the tallest trees in the Wishing Wood and she had longed to go inside it.

"Follow me," said Mistress Pipit, and set off with a line of eager fairies scurrying behind her. Lila couldn't have been happier and, chattering gaily, the three friends followed the other fairies through the trees of the Wishing Wood. Above them, the ancient oaks spread their mighty branches, shading out the sun, while long, sinewy roots anchored the great trunks to the earth.

"Keep to the path," Mistress Pipit called back.

"It's rather gloomy, isn't it?" Meggie said. "It feels as though that escaped wellipede might drop from one of the branches at any minute."

"It won't," said Bella. "Wellipedes are no good at climbing. It's podbugs that leap into things."

"Pipity isn't going to make us fly to the very top of the Flutter Tower, is she?" Meggie asked. "Heights make me dizzy. Even looking out of our bedroom window makes me freeze! There, I've said it."

"Dizzy!" said Bella as if she couldn't believe her ears. "But fairies have to fly high, that's what we do. In Year Five we'll be learning to collect stardust."

"I know," Meggie said, miserably. "But maybe by then I won't be so frightened. I just don't want to have to go too high in the Flying Test! That's all."

Ahead of them, Princess Bee Balm whispered something in Sea Holly's ear. Both fairies glanced back and giggled.

"Butterburs and bodkins," grimaced Lila. "Bee Balm's eavesdropping again!"

Waiting until the Princess and Sea Holly were out of hearing, Bella continued. "Meggie, how can you possibly be scared of heights? Flying high and free is fantastic fun."

"Bella!" scolded Lila. "Just because you're the sporty type and not scared of anything! Meggie may not like heights but she's good at lots of other things."

The sky-blue fairy looked sheepish.

"You mustn't worry about the test, Meggie," Lila said. "We'll do lots and lots of practice."

Ahead, Mistress Pipit stopped and turned to the fairies following her. "I'd like you all to listen carefully," she said. "The Wishing Wood is full of pathways and until you've learned them you must keep together. We're on one of the main routes, but here, at this oak tree, the path forks. The left path eventually takes you back to the Bugs and

Butterflies ring, where we were earlier. Don't use this path if you're in a hurry."

"That's for sure," whispered Bella, who knew the pathways like the back of her hand.

"The right fork leads to the Flutter Tower. Now, keep together. Bella and Lila, please can you stay at the back and make sure nobody goes the wrong way."

"Hey, Meggie, stay with us," Bella said.

"I can't think why you'd want her to," said Bee Balm. "A fairy who doesn't like heights isn't much of a fairy, is she?"

"A princess should be above making unpleasant remarks," said Lila, jumping in. "Don't you want your subjects to be loyal to you if you become queen?"

"It's not *if* I become queen but *when*, Lilac Blossom," said Bee Balm, ignoring the important part of what Lila had said. "Now tootle to the back of the line you three, where you belong."

"She is such a snob," said Bella, making a face behind the Princess's back.

The path ahead twisted and turned and sunlight dappled their way. Birds sang merrily in the trees, red squirrels jumped from branch to branch, and nobody got left behind. At last, Charm One Class arrived at the base of a glittering silver tower.

To find out what
happens next, read

Silverlake
Fairy School
Ready to Fly

Join Lila and her friends
for more magical adventures at

Silverlake Fairy School

Unicorn Dreams

Lila longs to go to Silverlake Fairy School to learn
about wands, charms and fairy magic – but
spoiled Princess Bee Balm is set on ruining Lila's
chances! Luckily nothing can stop Lila from
following her dreams...

Ready to Fly

Lila and her friends love learning to fly at Silverlake
Fairy School. Their lessons in the Flutter Tower are a
little scary but fantastic fun. Then someone plays a
trick on Lila and she's grounded. Only Princess Bee
Balm would be so mean. But how can Lila prove it?

Stardust Surprise

Stardust is the most magical element in the
fairy world. In fact, it's so powerful that all fairies at
Silverlake Fairy School are forbidden to use it by
themselves. But Princess Bee Balm will stop at
nothing to boost her magic...

Bugs and Butterflies

Lila dreams of being picked to play for her clan's Bugs
and Butterflies team, and she has a good chance, too,
until someone starts cheating! Princess Bee Balm is
being friendly to Lila too...so what's going on?

Dancing Magic

It's the end of term at Silverlake Fairy School, and Lila
and her friends are practicing to put on a spectacular
show. There's also a wonderful surprise in store for
Lila – one she didn't dare dream was possible!

www.silverlakefairyschool.com

About the Author

Elizabeth Lindsay trained as a drama teacher before becoming a puppeteer on children's television. Elizabeth has published over thirty books, as well as writing numerous radio and television scripts including episodes of *The Hoobs*. Elizabeth dreams up adventures for Lilac Blossom from her attic in Gloucestershire, where she enjoys fairytale views down to the River Severn valley. If Elizabeth could go to Silverlake Fairy School, she would like a silver wand with a star at its tip, as she'd hope to be with Lila in the Star Clan. Like Lila, Elizabeth's favorite color is purple.